Shogomoc Sam

SHOGOMOC SAM

Lorrie McLaughlin

Illustrated by Randy Jones

ST. MARTIN'S PRESS
NEW YORK

Library of Congress Catalogue Card No. 76-119017

Printed in Canada
for The Macmillan Company of Canada Limited
70 Bond Street, Toronto

Contents

The Main John

. . . Don't you hear them coming,
Tramping down the Glen?
Husky, lusty giants,
Shades of Glazier's men? . . .

They sing songs about them and they tell stories about them and when the lone moose calls along the shores of the Squatook Lake and the Tobique's white with foam, they remember how it used to be . . .

The Main John is a loggin' man from the very first, they'll tell you. He's a stream-driver when he isn't any more than seventeen and he nearly loses his life doin' it.

"You want to see stream-driving?" shouts the Main John. "I'll show you stream-driving!"

And he shows them, right enough, though he takes a header into deep water doin' it. He bobs to the surface, the Main John does, and the current sweeps him along and a log hits him on the head and knocks the breath out of him.

They haul the Main John ashore, shakin' their heads and sayin', "It's the end of the lad, sure enough."

One of the loggers shouts, "It takes more than a faceful of the Shogomoc to drown a loggin' man!" and he picks up the Main John and shakes out the water and says, "Give him a minute and you'll see how hard it is to kill a loggin' man!"

And sure enough, after a minute or two, the Main John blinks a bit and opens his eyes and the first thing he says is, "I told you I could stream-drive, didn't I?" and back he goes again.

The rivers and the logs and the stream-drivin' couldn't keep the Main John down, but the typhoid nearly does.

"He's done for this time, sure enough," they say up and down the loggin' camps in New Brunswick. "The typhoid's got him – and him only eighteen!"

"Takes more than the typhoid to finish off a loggin' man," says one of them.

And he knows what he's sayin', too, because the Main grits his teeth and hangs on and he fights that fever and he beats it. He loses his hair in the winnin', though, but before the logs are cut he's back in the woods with his peavey hook and his double-blade axe in his hands, and a bushy black wig and a stovepipe hat on his head.

The Main John's everywhere at once after that, it seems. He's wadin' in the icy waters of the Shogomoc with his coat-tails billowin' out behind him, and he's runnin' up and down the shore of the Tobique, shoutin' orders, and he's roarin' at the men up by Grand Falls, and grabbin' a peavey or a boat-hook when he has need of them.

"The Main John and his men are loggin' men, if ever there were any," they say in Fredericton and Saint John, and they sing songs about them and they tell stories about them and they remember how it used to be.

Sam, Sam, What a Shame ...

He ran down the dusty road, his schoolbooks dangling from the leather strap he had fastened around them, his head up, staring at a point somewhere beyond. Behind him wound the straggling trail of boys and girls, their chant rising and falling.

"Sam, Sam! What a shame! Nobody knows your name!
Sam, Sam! What a shame! Nobody knows your name!"

The voices grew louder as he passed the bent willow tree at the fork in the road and he slowed and almost stopped. He could turn and face them now, then run for home. But a bloodied nose would not stop the chant forever and a torn shirt would only make his mother sigh as she searched for a needle and thread.

Sam turned off at the fork and began to run across the fields, jumping the creek at its narrow point and ducking through the hole in the hedge of blueberry bushes.

And then he was home, at the small frame house that had stood unpainted for so many years that no one knew, any more, what colour it had once been. He dropped his books on the back stoop and went into the kitchen.

His mother was at the stove, stirring something in the big black kettle. He sniffed. Chowder.

"Fresh bread on the shelf," said his mother without turning around. "Bring your books in from the stoop or you'll be losing them again."

"In a minute, Ma," he said.

His mother turned and looked at him, her eyes wide with surprise. "It's not like you to talk back, Sam."

"At the school today," he said. He took a deep breath. "At school today teacher said for us to tell her what our folks did and what our grandfolks did, too."

His mother stirred the kettle of chowder and said nothing at all.

"When it got to be my turn I said that my pa worked in the lumber camps winter and spring and farmed some in the summers and that I didn't rightly know what my grandfolks had done." He ran his finger along the crack in the table top.

His mother still stirred the kettle of chowder and said nothing at all, but her shoulders seemed to stiffen and a

faint redness began to colour the back of her neck, just below the brown bun of hair.

"And somebody at the back of the room said I didn't know my folks, either, when it came right down to it, and that I had no real right to the name Campeau, and teacher said for him to sit down and speak when spoken to."

His mother banged the spoon down on the shiny black top of the cookstove and turned around. She sighed once, and sat in the rocking chair.

"I suppose it had to come sooner or later," she said. "There's no secret that keeps forever – least of all around these parts." Her voice sounded tight and angry. "Your name's Campeau because we say it is. We gave you the name, right and proper. You had a first name but you didn't have a last one, so we gave you ours. It's as simple as that, Sam." She stood up and went back to the stove. "There's the fresh bread on the shelf."

"I want to know," said Sam. "I want to know more than that."

"What good does knowing do?" demanded his mother. "What does knowing change?" She looked around the kitchen. "I wish your pa was here. He'd fix them for yelling at you. I wish your pa was here, instead of in town."

"Fixing them for yelling at me won't help," said Sam. "I want to know."

"Your pa found you," said his mother. "Wrapped up like a fancy present you were and tucked in a canoe on the banks of the Shogomoc. Your pa brought you home to me, like a man would bring flowers or candy or a bonnet, wrapped up like a fancy present, and he said you'd keep me company while he was logging. Your pa carried you all the way home from the Shogomoc."

"Didn't you ever try to find my folks?" asked Sam, still staring at the crack.

"We tried," said his mother. "But whoever wrapped you up snug and fancy didn't want to be found. There wasn't anything with you but a scrap of paper with your name on it – Sam. That's all."

"You should have told me before," he said.

His mother shook her head. "What would have been the good of that? You're ours by rights, same as if you were born to us." She looked worried. "You don't feel differently, do you? About your pa and me? You're ours by rights, Sam. You couldn't be more ours if you'd been born a Campeau."

"I don't feel differently," said Sam. "But I wish I'd been told. It seems like the sort of thing that ought to be told." He stood up and went out to the stoop to pick up his books. He did not go back into the kitchen, though. Instead, he walked over behind the barn and sat down on the old tree stump his pa used as a bench and stared across the field.

He could not remember ever having seen anything else. The small, stony pasture had always been there, with one cow or another grazing. Beyond it there had always been the tumbledown house where the Johnsons lived, and beyond that the road leading to school and then to town. He had never seen anything else and he could not imagine there being anything else.

But there had been something else. For a little while, on the banks of the Shogomoc, he had been somebody else. His pa and the lumberjacks went north every autumn and he had grown up thinking that some day he would go, too, because that was what men did. But he had already been there, once, long before. He began scratching figures in the dirt.

1850, he wrote.

And beneath that, 12.

He drew a line and wrote 1838.

That was when he'd been at the Shogomoc. It had begun there, fifty miles or more away. He rubbed his foot across the figures in the dirt, blotting them out. He closed his eyes, trying to imagine what the Shogomoc had been like. All he knew was what his pa had told him. Brilliant blue water and brilliant blue sky and trees touching the clouds.

He started slowly back to the house. His folks were sitting on the stoop, watching him as he walked. His mother started toward him, wiping her hands on her apron, then touching him lightly on the shoulder. "You shouldn't have gone off like that, without a word. I thought . . ." She shrugged and wiped her hands again.

Sam glanced at her and then away. There was still a worried look in her eyes and he was certain that she had thought he had run away.

"I wouldn't do that," he said. "I wouldn't leave without a good-bye."

"The Shogomoc's just a river," said his mother. "There's nothing special about it, is there, Josh?"

"Just a river," agreed his father. "And rivers change in twelve years, Sam. Just the way folks do. After twelve years, I couldn't even find the spot where I found that canoe."

Sam sat down on the stoop beside his folks as he had so many times in the past. He did not say anything more about the Shogomoc – but he did not stop thinking about it.

It was the last waking thought he had before he fell asleep that night, and in the morning, before he had fully opened his eyes, the word was going softly around in his brain. Shogomoc. Shogomoc.

Before school had even begun, he had bloodied two noses and shoved Sarah Johnson sprawling in the mud by the pump. He stood, fists raised, glaring at them all, until their chant, "Sam, Sam! What a shame!" faded into silence and then, as the school bell began to ring, he turned and ran down the road.

Behind him he could hear them shouting, "Sam! Sam, come back. You'll catch it!" But he did not stop running until he was far beyond the school, well on the way to Fredericton. He was not sure where he was going, only that he was going away from the chanting.

He went down to the river, finally, and stood watching the stevedores as they loaded the bales and barrels and boxes. Their shouts mingled with the shrill whistles of the tugs and the sudden loud hiss of steam let off from a boiler.

"Out of the way, boy!" shouted a workman. He shoved Sam to one side and hurried down to a rowboat, already loaded with passengers for one of the steamers.

Sam dug his hands deep into his empty pockets. If he had money, he could go out to one of the steamers and be off to Saint John or even beyond. But he had no money and no prospect of any, and sooner or later he would have to go home and face up to the bloodied noses and Sarah Johnson's muddied dress and the lessons he was missing.

He started away from the docks, looking back over his shoulder as he walked. He stumbled over a piece of board and a grey-haired man shouted, "Watch it, boy!" and held out a hand to keep him from falling.

"I suppose you want to be a sailor," said the old man. "Or a lumberjack."

"I want to be anything that gets me away from here and up to the Shogomoc," said Sam.

"The Shogomoc's not magic," said the old man. "And there are rivers that are bigger and rivers that are faster." He shrugged his shoulders. "No accounting for what people want, though. Sometimes it's the name of a river that catches their fancy and sometimes it's an idea, my boy." He looked at Sam. "You're no smaller than many who've gone into the woods and the Main John is looking for men now."

Sam did not have to ask who the Main John was. He knew. Even if his pa hadn't been a lumberjack, he'd have known. The Main John Glazier was known up and down the St. John River and some folks said he was known in lumber camps half across the country, too. Sam had never seen him – but he'd heard about him, for as long as he could remember.

How the Main John Got His Name

The Main John is a loggin' man from the moment he breathes his first breath and he'll be a loggin' man until he breathes his last. They say that when the Main John was born his pa takes one look at the lad and says, "Cut me down the tallest tree in New Brunswick and give it to the lad for a teething ring."

So the men go out, one after the other, lookin' for a tree tall enough and fine enough for the Main John to be cuttin' his teeth on and finally they bring back the tallest tree in the world and drop it down beside him.

The Main John looks at it and he puts his hands around it and his pa shouts out, "That's a teethin' ring meant for a loggin' man, if ever I saw one!"

And before anyone so much as blinks an eye, the Main John chews that log into toothpicks and spits them out in as neat a pile as ever any man had seen.

"He's a loggin' man, sure enough," says the Main John's pa and he tosses his two-bladed axe into the trunk of a tree. "No man's to be touching that axe except the boy here, when he's ready."

The axe stays there in the tree, waitin', and every once in a while some smart lumberjack comes along, thinkin' the axe is meant for him, but try as they do, none of them ever so much as budges it in the back.

"See," says the men who were there the day the Main John was born, "it's meant for the lad and nobody else!"

When the Main John is four or so, he decides it's time he set to work like everybody else and he starts through the woods, lookin' for the spot where his pa sank that axe. He finds it right off, too, because he's got a way in the woods and he's not one to get himself lost, the Main John isn't.

He stands there, lookin' at his pa's axe, and one of the lumberjacks who tried to pull out the axe and couldn't starts in laughin'.

"Back to the nursery, lad," he shouts. "Loggin' is work for men!"

The Main John looks as if he didn't even hear. He spits on his hands and he grabs hold of that axe handle and he gives it a pull that heaves up the tree and the earth around it so as there's a mountain where there never was one before, and he stands there with his pa's axe in his hand, shoutin', "Loggin' is work for *me*!" and there's not a man in the woods ready to argue the point with him.

After that, the Main John goes through the woods of New Brunswick like a buzz saw and by the time he's five or thereabouts, he's usin' a man's peavey hook and an axe as big as he is and there's not a tree in the forest he can't be cuttin' down with one swing.

There's not a man or a tree can stand in the way of the Main John and when he makes up his mind he wants a thing, it's as good as his.

"I think I'd like me some pancakes," he says one mornin' to the cook.

The cook thinks about it a bit and says, "That's all well and good but I don't have me a fry pan big enough to make pancakes to suit you!"

The Main John thinks about that for a second or so and then he shouts out for a fry pan bigger than any in the world. "No matter what it costs!" he shouts. "Get me a fry pan big enough to cook all the pancakes I can manage."

The cook starts runnin' as soon as the Main John starts to shout and he doesn't stop runnin' until he gets to Fredericton.

"I need me a fry pan!" he shouts. "Big enough to cook all the pancakes in the world!"

Nobody in town has ever seen a fry pan *that* big and the cook gets pretty upset because he knows he doesn't dare go back to the Main John without that fry pan. He runs all around Fredericton, shoutin' and lookin', and finally he spots a battleship anchored in the harbour.

The cook takes a look at that battleship and all its metal hull and its smokestacks risin' into the sky.

"That's what it takes to make a fry pan big enough to fry up all the pancakes in the world!" says the cook and before anybody knows what he's up to he starts shoutin' for all the loggin' men in town to give him a hand.

They work all day and all night, tearin' that battleship apart with their bare hands, and by dawn they've got the biggest fry pan anybody has ever seen, and they start in carryin' it back to the Main John.

Then everybody stands around while the cook starts mixin' up the batter and pourin' those pancakes out of a boiler and nobody watches closer than the Main John himself.

He starts eatin' those pancakes as soon as they're cooked, and by the next mornin' he's startin' to slow down a bit, and by sundown he says, "Now, that's what I call a man-sized servin' of pancakes! You can fry me up a second helpin'!"

Somebody new to those parts looks at the Main John, not quite believin' what he sees, and he says, "No man livin' can eat that many pancakes!"

The cook hardly looks up from mixin' up the second servin' of pancakes but somebody else shouts, "John Glazier can!"

"John who?" demands the fellow new to those parts and before anybody else can say a word the Main John turns and looks at him.

"*I'm* who!" he says. "John Glazier. The Main John!"

The loggers standin' around watchin' and listenin' nod their heads. "That's just who he is," they say. "The Main John!" and from then on nobody ever calls him anything else.

Cookie Sam

Sam looked at the old man but he was seeing far beyond the noisy dock. He could almost see himself on a drive with the Main John, peavey hook in hand, going beyond the Shogomoc to the sound of crosscut saws and axes and roaring rivers. Then he blinked and said, "My folks wouldn't want me to go. Not yet."

"I'm not one to tell you to say a never-you-mind to what your folks want," said the old man. He half-raised his hand in a wave and went off along the dock. He stopped once, though, to call back, "When you *do* go, lad, the Main John's the one to be going with!"

Sam nodded and went slowly down the road. He was beginning to get hungry and he thought about the lunch bucket he had dropped by the pump in the schoolyard, almost able to taste the thick slices of bread and meat.

Then he forgot his hunger.

There was a sudden shout and some catcalls from a crowd of men down at the corner of the dusty road. Two men ahead of him began to run and Sam hurried after them, calling as he ran "What's happening? What's wrong?" but neither man stopped long enough to answer.

A lanky, mop-haired boy began to run, too, and he shouted over the din, "It's the Main John and Paddy McGarrity. I can see Paddy's red shirt from here!" He laughed and sprinted ahead so that Sam had to take two steps for every one of his to keep up.

The crowd had formed a tightly packed circle and Sam jumped up and down, trying to see over the shoulders of the men. He gave up jumping, finally, and pushed and shoved until he was at the front of the crowd.

He saw a tall man, all bone and muscle, wearing a bushy black wig topped by a stovepipe beaver hat, standing with his hands on his hips, glaring down at two men sprawled on the ground.

The Main John ignored the younger of the two men and shouted, "What are you up to now, Paddy McGarrity? Is there no end to what you'll do?" He shook his fist. "Get to your feet and come along with me before they send you to the guardhouse!"

Paddy McGarrity got slowly to his feet, slapping the dust from his red pants and his red flannel shirt. He ran his fingers through his red hair, ruffling it more than smoothing it, and clapped his old straw hat on the back of his head. He shook his fist once at the man still sprawled on the ground and went down the road behind the Main John.

The crowd of men separated then. A few of them trailed along behind Paddy McGarrity and the Main John but most of them clustered around the man still on the ground, asking, "What happened? What's the trouble?"

The man got to his feet, scowling. "What ever happens with Paddy McGarrity?" he demanded in an angry voice. He shoved past the crowd and hurried off toward the dock.

Sam stared after him for a minute, then began to run down the road after the men who were following the Main John and Paddy McGarrity.

Paddy turned around once or twice, scowling and shaking his fist at the men following him, but the Main John strode along, head up, looking neither to the right nor to the left. One by one the men turned back until only Sam was left, walking along a dozen or more yards behind Paddy and the Main John Glazier.

"What do you want?" shouted Paddy McGarrity, his face almost as red as his shirt.

The Main John stopped walking, then, and looked at Sam. "Don't look so frightened, lad. Paddy's bark is worse than his bite."

"I'm not frightened," said Sam. "And I'm following you

because there's not a man alive who knows more about the river than you do."

The Main John threw back his head and laughed. "Do you think that's the way to get yourself a job with me?" he shouted. "Flattery won't get you a thing, even though it's more truth than flattery!"

"My folks wouldn't want me taking a job yet," said Sam. "I just wanted to find out about the Shogomoc."

"It's a river," said the Main John. "And there are bigger rivers than the Shogomoc."

"I come from up there," said Sam. "My pa found me in a canoe, wrapped up like a fancy present, and took me home with him."

The Main John stopped laughing and looked at Sam more closely. "I've heard that Josh Campeau found a baby, a dozen or so years ago. If you're half the man that Josh is, you can have a job in my camps any time you come asking. That's the truth, isn't it, Paddy?"

Paddy grinned. "I can put him to work in my kitchen, and *that's* the truth!"

"I wanted to know about the Shogomoc," said Sam again. "If you know all about the river . . ."

"I know about the river," said the Main John. "But I don't know any more about you than Josh does. Stop worrying about the past, boy. It's the future that's important."

Sam sat down on a log by the side of the road and watched the Main John and Paddy McGarrity until they were out of sight. He sighed. He was hungry again – and there was a long walk home. He started back the way he had come. He hadn't solved any of his problems. If anything, he had added to them. He didn't know any more about the Shogomoc and now he had to face up to his folks.

He walked more slowly than ever and for a minute he thought about never going home at all. Then the gnawing of hunger made him start to run. Whether he was late or early getting home he'd have some explaining to do – and it would be easier to explain when he had some food in his stomach.

His mother was at the kitchen door, looking up and down the road, when he cut through the gap in the blueberry hedge. She ran toward him when she saw him, waving her apron and shouting.

"You've had me worried half to death. As if enough hasn't happened without you running off without a word."

"I'm sorry, Ma," began Sam. "But they shouted and called me names . . ."

"There's more to worry about now than names and taunts," said his mother, half pulling him toward the house. "Your pa's lying in bed with his leg broken and the doctor's gone not ten minutes."

Sam began to run, too, and he was in the house before his mother had reached the stoop.

"What happened, Pa?" He ran toward the back bedroom.

His father looked up at him and shook his head. "I did what I'm always telling you not to do. I crossed the creek at the high point and went head first into the rocks."

Sam sat on the edge of the bed, staring at his father's bandaged and splinted leg, trying not to think of the months ahead. The farm wasn't rightly a farm at all; there was no money to be made from it. The cow and the market garden barely kept them in milk and vegetables. It was the money his father made each winter in the logging camps that kept them going from one year to the next, and his father would not be logging this year.

Each autumn, when his father and the other men went north to the logging camps, Sam stayed home with the women and the children. Each winter he dreamed of taking a peavey hook and an axe and going into the woods himself some day.

And now the day was here. For him, there would never be another time as right for logging as this time.

"The Main John Glazier offered me a job today," he said to his father. "And Paddy McGarrity said I could help him in the cookhouse." He waited.

He heard his mother make a small noise like a cry, but his father nodded. "There's not much choice about it now, Sam. I'd have had you wait a year or two if I'd had my way, but we can't be choosers now."

"I wanted to go anyway," said Sam. "From the time I found out about the Shogomoc and where I came from I've wanted to go, but I didn't feel right about leaving."

His father nodded in a tired way. "I know, Sam. There are some things I understand better than you think, I guess." He closed his eyes. "My peavey's behind the door, Sam. Take it along for luck."

Sam went out to the kitchen and picked up the peavey hook. He had held it many times before, closing his eyes and picturing himself in the woods. There was a different feel to it now, though, when he knew he was really on his way. Even if he was going to be a cookie or a handy man, he felt like a lumberjack with his father's peavey in his hand.

He stood at the kitchen door, staring along the road that led to Fredericton, thinking about how he would find the Main John and Paddy McGarrity.

"And I'll see the Shogomoc," he said to himself. "I'll find out who I am."

Sam's hopes of seeing the Shogomoc and finding out something about his past were dismissed by Paddy McGarrity, though, with a shrug and a wave of his beefy hands.

"We're going beyond the Shogomoc," he said. "And beyond Grand Falls, too. The Main John's going to do what's never been done before." Then he clamped his mouth tightly shut and refused to say another word. When Sam pestered to know what it was they were going to do that had never been done before, Paddy McGarrity shook his fist and said, "Off with you. If you're going to do nothing but ask questions, get along with you! You're hired on as cookie, not to be pestering me with questions from sun-up till dark!"

One morning as Sam walked beside Paddy, he sighed and said, "I'd hoped to see the Shogomoc, and maybe find out something about . . ."

Before he could finish his sentence, though, Paddy muttered under his breath, "Shogomoc! Shogomoc! I'm that sick of hearing the word from you! Shogomoc Sam, that's what I should be calling you, my lad! It's all you think about!" He grinned and repeated, "Shogomoc Sam!"

Somehow the words did not sound like a taunt when Paddy McGarrity said them and Sam grinned back at the bandy-legged little man.

"You're thinking too much about the past, Sam," said Paddy. "That's not what will be making you great, you know." He jerked his head sideways, toward where the Main John was riding along on his mare, Bonnie Doone. "Do you think he's the Main John because of his name? Or because of his pa or his grandpa? He'd be the Main John if he'd been found in a palace – or in a canoe! He's the Main John because he's the best there is!"

Sam looked at the Main John and the high-stepping mare, Bonnie Doone. He'd never seen a horse like her.

"And no wonder," said Paddy McGarrity. "There *isn't* another horse like her!"

How the Main John Rode the Fastest Horse in the World

Once when the Main John is loggin' on the Tobique River, he says to Paddy McGarrity, the bull cook, "Paddy, I'm gettin' mighty sick and tired of walkin'. I think I'll find me a horse."

Paddy grins a grin so wide it almost splits his red face in half and he says, "Good luck to you, Main John," and he runs his fingers through his red hair. "Give it a bit of thought first, though, Main John."

So the Main John sits himself down by the cookhouse door and thinks for a spell. The Main John thinks about gettin' a horse for eleven days, eleven hours, and eleven minutes, and then he stands up and straightens his stovepipe hat and starts down the road, coverin' half a mile or more with every step.

The Main John walks all over New Brunswick by nightfall, lookin' at every horse there is. He looks at so many horses he begins thinkin' he'll never find one to his likin', but he isn't a man to get discouraged easy-like, so he keeps on lookin' all the next day, too.

"No sense makin' a horse trade 'less it's a good horse trade," says the Main John, and he keeps on walkin'.

Pretty soon the word goes around that the Main John is lookin' to find himself a horse and right away every horse-trader in the country figures how maybe this is his time to make a fortune and a bit of fame as well, 'cause they know the Main John is fixin' to buy a horse and isn't likely to be persnickety about price.

Those horse-traders bring out big horses and little horses

and middle-sized horses, but not one of them is what the Main John has in mind and he tells the horse-traders so.

"I want me a horse as fast as the wind and as pretty as a star in the sky," says the Main John, and he keeps on walkin' and he keeps on lookin'.

The Main John is walkin' down a sideroad, kickin' up such a cloud of dust that it makes the people in Arizona start figurin' that a dust storm is comin', and all the time he's walkin' the Main John is thinkin'.

All of a sudden-like, the Main John hears a noise. He stops walkin', and he stops thinkin', and he stands there, just listenin'.

"Sounds to me like the neighin' of a horse that's as fast as the wind," says the Main John. "And it sounds to me like that horse isn't very far away."

He listens some more and he figures some more and he reckons that horse can't be more than eleven hundred miles away at most and he knows *he* can cover that distance easy in about twenty-two steps.

So the Main John starts out, takin' extra-big steps 'cause he's in such a hurry, and in less time than it takes to tell, he gets to the barn where he figures the mare is.

The Main John goes up to the barn door in an offhand way as if he doesn't much care whether he gets him a horse or not. He opens the barn door a smidgen and sort of glances inside, still in an offhand way.

And then he sees the mare who's been doin' all that neighin' and soundin' as fast as the wind.

The Main John walks up to that mare and he puts his mouth close to her ear and he whispers in a voice like the roll of summer thunder, "What would they be callin' you, my bonnie girl?"

The mare neighs once and tosses her head in the air and the Main John bursts out laughin' so hard that folks down Tennessee way figure there's a hurricane a-comin'.

"Bonnie, that's what you are!" cries the Main John and right there on the spot he names the mare Bonnie Doone.

The Main John snaps his fingers, startin' an earthquake

in Greenland, and goes off to find the horse-trader.

The Main John finds that horse-trader 'round to the back of the barn, sittin' on a keg of nails, smokin' a pipe and waitin'.

"I want me a horse," says the Main John. "And the horse I want me the most is the mare in the barn."

"Maybe she's for sale and maybe she isn't," says the horse-trader, slow and easy-like, figurin' to himself that this is like as not the time to make him his fortune.

"She's for sale," says the Main John. He looks the horse-trader right in the eye and the horse-trader sort of quivers and shakes a bit. "She's for sale," says the Main John again, "isn't she?"

And the horse-trader nods his head and says, "She's for sale, right enough."

And that's how the Main John buys Bonnie Doone, without so much as askin' the price 'cause he knew, soon as he heard her neigh and took one look at her, that she's the fastest horse in the world.

The Main John tosses a saddle on Bonnie Doone and starts off, ridin' like the wind, and before he's any more than got started he's back in camp, laughin' down at Paddy McGarrity and shoutin' how he's ridden like the wind and covered half of New Brunswick in less than an hour.

"No horse livin' can do that, Main John," shouts somebody, and before the words are even out of his mouth the Main John snatches him up and rides off, clear around New Brunswick and back again.

"There!" shouts the Main John, droppin' the fellow down on the ground again. "Is my Bonnie Doone the fastest horse in the world or isn't she?"

And the fellow just stands there, too out of breath and upset to say anything, and finally he just nods his head in a tired sort of way, him not being used to ridin' around New Brunswick in the flick of an eyelash.

"That's what you are!" cries the Main John to Bonnie Doone. "The fastest horse in the world! And nobody's ever goin' to be doubtin' it again!"

And nobody ever does doubt it again! Up and down the length and breadth of New Brunswick – and maybe Maine and Quebec, too – the talk is that the Main John's mare, Bonnie Doone, is the fastest horse in the world.

Trouble Ahead

Sam helped cook up the porridge in the mornings and he scoured out the pots afterwards and he listened to the men talk about the logs that were being cut.

"I could use a peavey," he said to Paddy McGarrity.

"Sure, and we all could," said Paddy McGarrity. "But who else can cook porridge and scour out the pots but you and me?"

"I came along to be a logger," said Sam, "and to find out about the Shogomoc and all I'm doing is cooking."

Paddy McGarrity banged down his spoon and glared at Sam. "All you're doing is cooking," he said. "*All* you're doing! You're doing a good bit more, if you ask me! You're talking too much for one thing, and complaining too much for another!" His face turned almost as red as his hair and he shoved his old straw hat to the back of his head. "*All* you're doing is cooking! And where would the log-drive be, I'd like to know, without the likes of you and me to put the beans in the pot and the pork in the beans?"

Sam looked at Paddy McGarrity and said nothing at all. He'd been cookie long enough to know that if he argued or tried to explain Paddy's face would grow redder and redder and his eyes would flash with anger.

After a minute, Paddy banged down a black cooking pot and said, "Out you go. I don't want to share my kitchen with *you* this morning!"

Sam walked towards the door, still not saying anything at all. He'd been put out of Paddy's kitchen before and he knew that by supper-time it would all be forgotten.

"And don't think you're going to get out of cooking the supper beans!" Paddy McGarrity called after him.

Sam walked along the dirt path, scuffing the twigs and stones beneath his feet. The loggers were deep in the woods, but now and then he thought he could hear a shout or the ring of an axe.

If he went after them . . .

If he asked the Main John . . .

He sighed. It wouldn't do any good. He'd been hired on as cookie and handy man and it had begun to look as if he'd never get the chance to use his father's peavey.

He walked across the bumpy ground to the bunkhouse and listened to the sounds of the men. He sat on his hard, narrow cot and sniffed the familiar smells of rubber boots and yesterday's beans and tobacco and thought about the Shogomoc.

Once, on the way north, Paddy McGarrity had waved a beefy hand and pointed. "Shogomoc's that way, Sam. But there's nothing there for logging men now. We're going beyond Grand Falls, where the likes of us have never been before! That's what you have to be thinking about, Sam!"

Sam kicked the leg of the table. Well, he was beyond Grand Falls now and sometimes in the stillness of early morning he could hear the roar of the water as it plunged over the cliffs to pound on the rocks in the narrow gorge below.

Sam went back to the cookhouse, finally, walking slowly because he wasn't certain that Paddy would want to see him. When he opened the door, though, and saw Paddy sitting on a chair, his feet propped on the table, he cleared his throat.

"Well, I'm back," he said.

Paddy puffed on his pipe and blew a ring of smoke into the air. "So you are," he said. He jerked his head toward the old black cookstove. "I'm making doughnuts for supper and it looks to me as if they're extra-fine ones. What do you think?"

Sam went over and looked at the heavy black pot full of bubbling fat. He pulled one of the doughnuts out with the long-handled fork.

He took a bite and looked across at Paddy McGarrity.

"Well?" demanded Paddy. "Did you ever taste a better doughnut than that?"

Sam took another bite. It was greasy and heavy and doughy and not at all like the doughnuts his mother had made. "They're the best doughnuts you've ever made, Paddy," he said finally.

"Have another one, then, if you like," said Paddy, in a pleased way. "And then you can toss a bit of pork into the beans. Not too much, though, mind you!"

Sam nodded and took two pieces of salt pork from the supply bin. He began cutting it into cubes while Paddy watched him. When he reached for a third strip of meat, Paddy grunted.

"Two's more than enough, Sam," said Paddy. "We don't want to go spoiling the men, do we? After all, they're having doughnuts for supper!" He put the third strip of meat back in the supply bin. "Time enough for extras at Christmas or thereabouts!"

"What will we really have for Christmas, Paddy?" asked Sam.

Paddy looked surprised. "Extra pork in the beans," he said. "Maybe fried pork and molasses for breakfast – or buckwheat cakes, if you've a mind to make them." He laughed. "And pie. Blueberry or apple, Sam. Take your pick. I've got them both dried and waiting."

"It won't seem much like Christmas," said Sam.

Paddy shrugged. "The time to be celebrating is when you're back in Fredericton, Sam. If you're going to be a logging man, you learn to make do. And part of the learning to make do is thinking more about work than about holidays." He poked Sam in the ribs. "By the time Christmas comes you'll be such a logging man you won't even be looking at the calendar!"

"I'll be looking," said Sam.

But the days began to run into each other and sometimes he wasn't quite sure whether it was Tuesday or Wednesday and by the time December had turned into January he couldn't remember whether they'd had fried pork and molasses or buckwheat cakes for breakfast.

The logs piled up along the Allagash and the snow began to melt from the roof of the cookhouse. More and more often, Paddy McGarrity stuck his head out of the door and sniffed.

"Spring is coming, Sam," he said. "I can smell it and I can feel it and before you know it we'll be running the logs down the Allagash to the Grand Falls."

"What will we do then, Paddy? They say in the bunkhouse there's not a man living who gets logs over the Grand Falls and that the Main John won't be able to do it, either."

Paddy shrugged. "I've known the Main John more years than you've lived, Sam, and I've never known him not to be able to do what he sets out to do."

"They say he won't be able to run logs over the Grand Falls, Paddy," argued Sam. "They say if he does it, he'll do it alone!"

Paddy looked at Sam and his face began to get red. "That's what they say, is it?" he demanded. "The Main John stands to win or lose everything on these logs, Sam. He'll get them over the Grand Falls if he has to do it himself!" He went over to the cookstove and began banging the pots and pans around.

One morning when Sam went to the cookhouse, he found Paddy McGarrity whistling while he worked.

"Buckwheats for breakfast, Sam," sang out Paddy. "And fried pork and molasses as well! Do you know what that means?"

Sam shook his head and looked at the pile of buckwheat pancakes. He knew they'd be tough and leathery the way they always were, but he was so hungry he didn't really care.

"It means spring!" said Paddy McGarrity. He shook his spoon in the air. "It means spring and the start of the log drive and before you know it we'll be back in Fredericton with money in our pockets, that's what it means!" He began to whistle again.

Sam turned around and went out of the cookhouse. He went over and sat on a tree stump and stared up at the sky. He sniffed the air the way Paddy had and for the first time it seemed to him that there was a different smell to it.

"Spring!" he said.

"Spring it is!" agreed the Main John from behind him.

Sam jumped to his feet and started back to the cookhouse, but before he had gone more than a few steps the Main John caught him by the arm.

"What do you think of the drive, Sam? Do you fancy the life of a logging man?"

Sam hesitated. "I like it fine," he said finally. "But I didn't see the Shogomoc and I didn't find out what I set out to find!"

The Main John sighed. "Some of us never find out what we set out to find, Sam. And some of us change our minds about what we want to find out. What is it you wanted to find out, Sam?"

Sam looked surprised. "Who I am," he said, "That's what I set out to learn. Who I am."

"Don't you know?" demanded the Main John. "Don't you know who you are, Sam?"

Sam shook his head. "I don't know any more now than when I left Fredericton."

"Well," said the Main John, "maybe you'll find out by the time you get back to Fredericton." He looked up at the sky and said, half to himself, "You set out to find out who you are and I set out to make a fortune and who's to know what will happen to either one of us." He walked away and left Sam standing there.

Sam went slowly back to the cookhouse. "The Main John talked to me, Paddy," he said. "And if you ask me, he sounded worried."

Paddy shook his head and said, "He's got good reason to be worried, if you ask *me*. Millions of feet of logs waiting to be set free and him wondering how to get them beyond Grand Falls. It's enough to worry any man!" He snapped his fingers. "I'll cheer him up with an extra serving of buckwheats, that's what I'll do!" And he began slapping the thick, leathery pancakes onto a plate. "That's enough to cheer up any man living, isn't it, Sam?"

The St. John was at its highest in May and the first of the logs ran from the Allagash to Grand Falls in six hours.

"What do you think of that?" demanded Paddy McGarrity. "Two hundred miles in six hours! Who but the Main John could do it?"

Sam nodded without saying anything. He'd heard the

men in the bunkhouse talking for weeks and he knew they had no intention of running the logs over the Grand Falls for the Main John or anyone else!

"Nobody's ever driven timber over the Grand Falls," one of the loggers said. "It can't be done. Not by the Main John or anyone else, and I want no part of trying!"

The men sat around the cookhouse, not saying anything but just waiting.

The Main John looked at them. He straightened the stove-pipe hat on top of his head and he looked at them again. He took out his pipe and packed tobacco into it and then he sat down on the stump of a tree.

Paddy McGarrity nudged Sam in the ribs and whispered, "Keep your eyes open now, Sam. Something's going to happen, and that's for sure."

"I'm driving logs over the Grand Falls," said the Main John. "Who's going on the drive with me?"

The logging men stayed where they were, not saying anything. The only sound Sam could hear was the roar of the Grand Falls in the distance and the pounding of his own heart.

"Well?" said the Main John. "Who's going on the drive with me?"

One of the logging men cleared his throat. "It can't be done," he grumbled. "If we try it we'll be killed and the logs will be mashed to pulp on the rocks."

"Is nobody going on the drive with me?" shouted the Main John.

Paddy McGarrity muttered something and his face turned as red as his hair. He yanked off the dirty-grey apron he wore and threw it on the ground.

"I'll go with you," he shouted, shaking his fist. "It's you and me will run the logs over the Grand Falls and you and me who'll go down in history!"

Sam stared at Paddy McGarrity, standing red-faced and angry beside the Main John. He licked his dry lips and then he took a step forward, toward Paddy and the Main John.

"And me!" shouted Sam. "Me and my pa's peavey hook!"

The Main John stared at Sam, and Paddy McGarrity shouted, "What do you think of that, you scalawags! The boy and myself who never drove a log in our lives are ready to stand by the Main John! Oh, it's the laughing stock of New Brunswick you'll be when we get back to Fredericton!"

"Back to your fry pan, Paddy McGarrity," shouted one of the logging men. "And take the boy with you! I'm with the Main John. If he says the Falls can be drove, then I'll drive them!"

"And I'll help you!" shouted a second man.

"And me!"

"And me!"

"And me!"

The Main John nodded and looked pleased with himself. "We'll do what's never been done before, lads!" he shouted. "They'll be singing songs and telling tales about us and how we ran the logs over the Grand Falls."

"And that's a fact!" cried Paddy McGarrity. "And there's extra buckwheats for breakfast!"

Paddy McGarrity and Sam went back to the cookhouse and began frying extra pancakes.

"I wish I could have gone on the drive," said Sam. "Don't you, Paddy?"

Paddy shook his head. "I'll do anything for the Main John," he said. "And if I have to, I'll drive logs, but given my choice I'll stay in my cookhouse making buckwheats fit for a king!"

How the Main John Found Paddy McGarrity

They say in the loggin' camps that there's nothing Paddy McGarrity won't be doin' for the Main John Glazier and that if he was only the cook he thinks he is there wouldn't be better-fed loggers anywhere in the world.

"Paddy's a talker and Paddy's a fighter," the loggin' men say, "but Paddy's no cook, and that's a fact!"

But some of the loggin' men shook their heads. "The Main John says Paddy McGarrity's a cook," they say, "and that sure enough makes him one!"

And they start in laughin' and rememberin' how the Main John finds Paddy McGarrity.

The Main John has been ridin' the mare, Bonnie Doone, all over the world, findin' trees that had to be logged. He's been out west and logged every tree in sight and made the Great Plains and then he's gone beyond that and shoved up the dirt into piles and made the Rockies and finally he's had enough of travellin' and he's ridden back to New Brunswick where he belongs.

The Main John is ridin' down the street of Fredericton one day, feelin' the sun on his face and thinkin' about what to do next when he hears this shoutin' and commotion. When he looks up he can hardly believe his eyes.

There, astride a big grey horse, he sees a man. A bandy-legged, ham-fisted, red-faced man. A man with a mop of red hair sticking through the holes in the crown of his old straw hat. A man wearin' pants as red as his hair and a shirt that's even redder.

"I'm the king of all I see!" shouts the red-haired man on

the horse. "There's not a man livin' or breathin' or walkin' had better get in *my* way, and that's a fact!"

"You'd better get out of the way, Paddy McGarrity!" shouts somebody from the side of the road. "The troops are parading down this road and you'd better get out of their way!"

Paddy McGarrity shouts, "I'll not be getting out of the way of any man marching!" and there he stays, smack in the middle of the road.

The troops come marchin', right enough, down the centre of the road, straight toward Paddy McGarrity.

"I won't be moving an inch," shouts Paddy, waving his old straw hat in the air.

He digs his heels into his horse and starts ridin' toward the troops, shoutin' out how it's his road, right enough, and there's nothin' will move him.

"Out of my way, you spalpeens!" shouts Paddy McGarrity, and he heads his horse for the troops.

The troops stand fast, though, and the big grey horse stops in his tracks and Paddy McGarrity goes head over heels in the air and lands on the ground with a crash you could hear clear across to Maine.

The troops scoop up Paddy McGarrity as if he is a sack of potatoes and they carry him off to the guardhouse and put him on a diet of bread and water.

The Main John watches them until they are out of sight and then he leans over and says to Bonnie Doone, "What did you think of Paddy McGarrity, my bonnie girl?", and the mare tosses her head and whinnies a bit. "Exactly how I feel, my girl!" says the Main John, and he rides down the road after the troops.

The Main John talks to this one and he talks to that one and he pays a fine or two and then he goes to see Paddy McGarrity.

"What can you do, Paddy McGarrity?" demands the Main John. "Maybe I can use a man like you in the camps!"

"I can lay bricks," says Paddy McGarrity.

The Main John laughs. "I don't have much need for bricklaying in the camps, Paddy McGarrity."

"I can do a bit of barberin'," says Paddy McGarrity.

The Main John laughs again. "And I don't have need for barbering in the camps, Paddy McGarrity."

Paddy McGarrity thinks a bit. "What do you have need of in the lumbering camps?" he demands.

"A cook!" says the Main John.

"I can cook," says Paddy McGarrity. "And that's a fact!"

"Then you're hired," shouts the Main John.

And *that's* how the Main John hires Paddy McGarrity and gets himself a cook who doesn't know a stove from a fry pan and who makes doughnuts that sink to the bottom of a mug of coffee faster than a bullet leaves a rifle.

"I can cook!" shouts Paddy McGarrity. "And that's a fact!" and he glares at the loggin' men daring them to argue the fact with him, and none of them do because the Main John laughs and says, "If you say you're a cook, Paddy McGarrity, then that's what you are!", and there's not a loggin' man breathin' who's ready to argue with the Main John.

Into the Woods

The drive started next morning. Paddy and Sam stood on the banks of the river, watching.

"You're seeing something no man has seen before," said Paddy McGarrity as the pine logs shot over the Grand Falls. "Didn't I tell you, months ago, that there were more important things than the Shogomoc! You're making history, lad!"

Sam nodded, too busy watching the pounding logs to listen to what Paddy was saying. He had never in his life seen anything to equal it, and for the first time he began to understand the way his father felt about logging. There was something about the roar of the Falls, the rushing of the logs heading downriver for the booms near Fredericton, that made everything else seem unimportant.

"As long as the water level stays up, we're home free!" shouted Paddy. "The Main John will make his fortune this time for sure – and us with him! We'll be the proud ones, walking the streets of Fredericton, when this is over!"

The days seemed to run together after that, into an endless roar of logs heading downriver. The sound of the logs, and of the Falls, and of the lumberjacks shouting became so much a part of his day that Sam scarcely heard them.

Then one morning he awakened to a different sound. A sound he could not quite place. He hurried over to the cookhouse and found Paddy McGarrity sitting silently by the big black stove.

"What is it?" asked Sam. "What's wrong?"

Paddy sighed. "What's always wrong with logging men,"

he said. "River level is falling. It's always highest around May – and then it begins to fall. Logs that would have taken six hours from the Allagash take that many days now – and things will get slower before they get faster, Sam."

"But the logs will still get there," argued Sam. "We've been away since September. What does it matter if it takes a few weeks more."

"You're not a logging man, even if you do have your father's peavey hook," snapped Paddy. "That river's going to keep dropping and the logs are going to start to pile up along the gravel bars and the rocks and we'll have to leave them there."

Sam sat down beside Paddy without saying anything. He could remember one year when it was late September before his father came back from the drive. Josh Campeau had come into the house and said, "We had to wait for the river to rise with the autumn rain before we could get the logs moving again."

"We won't have to stay here until September, will we, Paddy?"

"I don't know what we'll have to do," said Paddy. "All I know is that we'll be doing whatever the Main John tells us to do." He stood up shaking his head. "What we're going to do right now, though, is get to work making an extra batch of wheatcakes. And I've a good mind to toss in a bit of fried pork and molasses as well. Nothing cheers a man up like a tasty meal, Sam!" He went over to the stove and began poking at the fire, a puzzled look on his face. "What bothers me is *why* the river's falling so fast. I've never seen it like this before. That's what bothers me, Sam – and I've got a hunch it's what bothers the Main John, too."

The Main John looked even more puzzled than Paddy McGarrity had that morning. He ate his wheatcakes all in a bite and then he went out of the cookhouse without saying anything to anybody. A minute later, Sam saw the Main

John ride off into the woods on Bonnie Doone, his coattails flying, his tall beaver hat clamped firmly on his head.

"Where do you suppose he's gone, Paddy?" asked Sam. "What's he going to do?"

"I don't know," admitted Paddy. He sounded a little bit cheerful for the first time that morning. "But wherever he's gone, he's going to be doing something about his logs, and that's a fact!"

The logs crept downriver toward the Falls all that day and as they began to stack up along the drying banks the lumberjacks shouted less and less.

"Not even salt pork for supper will cheer them up now," said Sam.

"Not even doughnuts will cheer them up!" agreed Paddy McGarrity. "I wish the Main John would come riding back. That's what I wish, and that's a fact!"

When the Main John finally rode back into camp, his jaw was set and his eyes were dark with anger.

"Oh, oh!" said Paddy McGarrity. "Something's up. I can tell by the tilt of the Main John's head! There's trouble brewing, and that's a fact!"

He walked out of the cookhouse, wiping his hands on his apron, and after a moment, Sam followed him. The Main John was standing in the centre of a circle of lumberjacks and not a man among them spoke a word. They just waited.

"Well," said the Main John. "It's not the falling river we have to be fighting this time, my boys!" He looked around at the silent circle of men. "It's what's making the river fall – that's what we have to be fighting!" He shook his fist in the air. "And what's making the river fall? Can you tell me that?" Again he waited while the silent circle of men watched him.

"What's making it fall, Main John?" shouted Paddy McGarrity, finally. "Why are the logs running aground all up and down the river instead of shooting over the Falls?"

"The lumberjacks in Maine are using our water!" shouted the Main John. "They've diverted the river, that's what they've done! They're using our water to float their logs and *that's* why we're not stream-driving this very minute!" He waited. "And what do you think of that?"

"I don't think much of it, and that's a fact!" cried Paddy McGarrity. He whipped off his apron and shook it in the air. "And I'm for doing something about it!"

One of the lumberjacks laughed. "What are you going to do, Paddy McGarrity? Throw some of your doughnuts at them, like cannon balls? Or hit them over their heads with one of your wheatcakes?"

Paddy scowled. "I'm going to be doing something!" he shouted.

"We're all going to be doing something," said the Main John.

The circle of lumberjacks muttered agreement and one of them called out, "What are we going to do, Main John?"

"They're along the Allagash, by Churchill Lake," said the Main John. "They've dammed up the river and built themselves up a head of water and they're using the Allagash as they see fit with never a thought for us and our logs!"

"Then let's go along the Allagash to Churchill Lake!" cried Paddy McGarrity, waving his apron. "Let's show them they can't treat New Brunswick men like this!"

"Are you ready to be soldiers, then, instead of lumbermen, for a change?" called the Main John.

"We're ready, Main John," shouted the men. "We're with you."

"Then get your peaveys and your axes," shouted the Main John. "And get the explosives!" He looked at Paddy McGarrity and Sam, standing by the door of the cookhouse.

"What about us, Main John?" called Paddy. "What about Shogomoc Sam and myself? Sam's got his pa's peavey and I've got a fist as strong as an axe."

"Why, you're coming along," said the Main John. "So step lively!"

Paddy tossed his apron on the floor of the cookhouse and tossed his straw hat in the air, and Sam ran over to the bunkhouse to get his father's peavey.

The lumberjacks started off in a ragged line, winding through the woods, their hobnailed boots thumping along the path as they walked. Sam and Paddy brought up the end of the line, and up ahead, through the trees, they could catch glimpses of the Main John and the others. The bright plaid shirts and the mackinaws, the gaudy pants the lumberjacks favoured, made bright splashes of colour, and some of the men were whistling as they walked.

"There's nothing a logging man likes more than a good set-to," said Paddy McGarrity to Sam. "You're a lucky boy to be along with the Main John and me this time! Logging over the Grand Falls for the first time! And if *that's* not enough, setting off to Maine to give those scalawags what for!"

They reached the banks of the Allagash, finally, below Churchill Lake, and Paddy McGarrity said, "This is it, my boy! Swing your peavey and keep your head low and good luck to you, Sam!"

The Main John let out a shout that could be heard up and down the river, and a moment later the woods seemed to be full of lumberjacks, swinging their peaveys and their fists and shouting as they fought.

Wherever Sam looked he saw the Main John, coattails flying, tall beaver hat clamped down on his head, and always, over the other shouts, he could hear the roar of Paddy McGarrity, "We're beating them, Sam! Swing that peavey and keep your head down!"

And then, finally, the Main John roared, "They're on the run, lads! We'll drive them clear through Maine and beyond!"

Later, the Main John and his men sat on tree stumps or

sprawled on the ground, laughing as they counted their blackened eyes or bruised knuckles, and when the Maine dam went up in a bang of explosives they let out a cheer that could be heard back in Fredericton.

"We've done it!" shouted Paddy McGarrity. "They'll be talking about this in logging camps around the world until the end of time, Sam! Oh, this is a story logging men will be telling for years to come!"

How the Main John Did What Had To Be Done

They say around the loggin' camps that the Main John is as peaceable as any man walkin', except when he gets riled, when, of course, he's somethin' else again.

And the Main John was bein' mighty peaceable, there by the Grand Falls, watchin' his logs run downriver, but when he finds out those scalawags in Maine have dammed up the water and are floatin' their logs downstream while his logs lie there like so many toothpicks, why, he gets angry, right enough.

The Main John goes off on Bonnie Doone to think things over, ridin' like the wind and talkin' as he rides, because Bonnie Doone isn't like any mare livin'.

"Bonnie Doone has a heart and a head," says the Main John, time and time again. "She's got more sense than most men livin', if you ask me!"

So the Main John rides around the world between sun-up and sundown, talkin' to Bonnie Doone and makin' up his mind what's to be done about those scalawags down in Maine.

"I have to get me my logs down to Fredericton," says the Main John.

Bonnie Doone tosses her head and whinnies a bit and the Main John tosses her a bit of sugar and rides on, still thinkin' and talkin'.

"So what's to be done, my bonnie girl?" asks the Main John and he doesn't even wait for an answer. "What's to be done is as clear as a New Brunswick sky," he says. "Blow up the dam, that's what's to be done. Blow up the dam and set my logs free to run the Falls and shoot down to Fredericton the way I planned for them to go!"

So the Main John gets his loggin' men together, decked out in their mackinaws and plaid pants and carryin' their peavey hooks and axes and ready to fight at the drop of a word. Not more than two dozen of them, there were, settin' off to take on a couple of hundred of Maine men and not battin' an eye at the odds because they knew they had the Main John at the lead and that *he* was the equal of any thousand men that ever carried an axe.

With the Main John shoutin' them on, they cover the miles of the forests as if it isn't more than a run from the bunkhouse to the cookhouse, singin' and laughin' all the way.

When they get to Churchill Lake the Main John lets out a shout like thunder that sets off tremors in mountains on the other side of the world. "Are you ready?"

"We're ready!" shout back his men, and the roar of their voices can be heard clear down in Saint John so that folks there prick up their ears and say to one another, "There's something going on somewhere!"

Those two dozen New Brunswick lumberjacks, with the Main John at the lead, rush down on a couple of hundred Maine jacks, shoutin' at the tops of their voices and wavin' their peaveys and swingin' their fists.

"It's the Main John and his men!" shouts one of the scalawags and he starts to run so fast he crashes into half a dozen of his friends and they all go down in a heap.

"They're on the run!" shouts the Main John in a voice like a thousand cannon, and when the Maine men hear *that* they snatch up their mackinaws and their axes and start runnin' and later on folks say they don't stop runnin' until they get to the Pacific and that *that's* how loggin' started out there!

When the Main John sees what's happenin', he starts to roar with laughter, and the roarin' of his voice is like the boomin' of fifty thousand cannon and it sets off such a tremblin' and shakin' in the earth that the dam those scalawags built goes up with a bang.

"Well," says the Main John, "I reckon we don't need those explosives we brought along after all!" and he laughs as he sees the water pourin' back down the river where it belongs.

Folks say that dam went up with such a bang that the river rose three feet in a second, down at the Grand Falls, close to two hundred miles away.

Maybe it did and maybe it didn't. Could have been that river rose somethin' more like two and a half feet. But however much it rose, the Main John's logs go shootin' over the

Grand Falls the way they were meant to shoot, and they shoot right on downstream to the booms faster than any logs ever shoot before.

When the Main John sees what's happenin' to his logs, he laughs a laugh that shakes the birds out of the treetops and makes folks in California think there's another earthquake comin'.

"We did it, boys!" shouts the Main John.

"We did it and that's a fact!" shouts Paddy McGarrity and the Main John leaps on the back of Bonnie Doone and rides clear around the world, just because he's feelin' so good!

Shogomoc Sam Comes Home

The logs swept off the river banks where they had run aground and shot over the Grand Falls. They poured down the river toward Fredericton and the Main John and his men followed them home.

For as long as he could remember, Sam had heard his father talk about the drive downriver to Fredericton and then beyond that to Saint John. Sometimes he thought he had heard the stories so many times that he knew every inch the logs would move but there was something different about being there on the drive, a part of it.

"It's like Pa said," he told Paddy McGarrity one morning as he watched the logs shooting downstream, as fast and as sure as if they were being shot from a rifle. "There's nothing like the Saint John drive!"

"That's a fact," agreed Paddy McGarrity. "There's not a town on the river doesn't owe its life to lumber. Nor a man on the river, either!"

The logs poured into the Springhill and Sugar Island booms for sorting and the rafts began to fill the river, until it seemed to Sam as if it was a sea of logs.

Paddy and Sam worked along with the men, and Paddy shouted instructions as he worked.

"Snub the rafts to the willows along the shore, Sam," he cried, fastening the rope as he shouted and then shaking his head impatiently when Sam's fingers were not quite as nimble as his own.

Later, though, when Sam snubbed a raft as neatly as Paddy had, the cook laughed and said, "Why, you're a

✓ Joe McTagart
✓ TOM Brown
✓ JUAN Milligan...
Shogomoc
Sam Car

lumber man, sure enough, Sam! Next year you'll be too handy to be helping me in the cookhouse. You'll be right there with the Main John, and that's a fact!"

Sam didn't say anything but he looked across at Paddy McGarrity and smiled.

Finally, the lumberjacks trailed into Fredericton, their faces dark from the sun, their mackinaws not quite as bright as when they'd left, and Sam and Paddy McGarrity walked with them.

"It's the end of the drive," said Paddy. "Here it began and here it ends and when the men are paid off they'll live like kings for a day or two and then they'll be back, asking the Main John to give them a job in the mills, like as not." He grinned. "And all the time they'll be waiting until it's time to head back up to the Grand Falls again."

Sam nodded and walked along beside Paddy, down the familiar streets of Fredericton, past the dock where he had first caught a glimpse of the Main John.

"You're awfully quiet, Sam," said Paddy. "Are you thinking about logging next year?" He waited a moment. "Or are you thinking about the Shogomoc?" He nudged Sam in the ribs. "Cheer up, lad. Maybe next year you'll see the Shogomoc and find out what you want to find out."

Sam looked at Paddy and then back toward the Main John, paying off his men. It had been a long time since he'd had time to think about the Shogomoc, he realized.

"I don't know what I'm thinking," he said to Paddy and he went over and stood in line behind the logging men, waiting for the money he'd earned.

"And who are you?" the Main John asked each of the lumberjacks in turn, laughing as he asked because he knew each man better than he knew the palm of his own hand.

When Sam got to the front of the line, he looked at the Main John and waited.

The Main John laughed and said, "And who are you?"

Sam didn't answer for a minute. He stood there, looking up at the Main John and thinking about all that had happened. He hadn't seen the Shogomoc and he didn't know any more about how he'd been found, wrapped up in a blanket, so long before. But it didn't seem to matter the way he had once felt it did.

"Who are you?" asked the Main John again and he had stopped laughing.

Sam looked at the Main John and then he looked over at Paddy McGarrity.

He straightened his shoulders. "Sam," he said. He looked the Main John straight in the eye. "Shogomoc Sam Campeau, that's who!" And he held out his hand for the pay he had earned.

"Shogomoc Sam Campeau," repeated the Main John, making a mark in his book. He counted out the money.

Sam signed his name in the book, writing firmly and carefully, the way he had been taught.

Shogomoc Sam Campeau.

He shoved his money into his pocket and waved to Paddy McGarrity.

Then he began to run, down the road toward home. He slowed when he reached the schoolhouse and saw Sarah Johnson by the pump, her pigtails neatly in place, her starched dress standing out around her.

"Sorry I pushed you in the mud!" shouted Sam.

Sarah Johnson looked at him and frowned in a puzzled way and turned away.

"It's me!" shouted Sam.

Sarah Johnson turned and looked at him again, the puzzled frown still on her face.

"Sam!" he said. "It's me! Shogomoc Sam Campeau!"

He didn't wait to hear what Sarah Johnson had to say. He began to run, faster than ever, down the road and across the field and through the gap in the blueberry hedge.

He began to shout, then. "Ma! Pa! It's me. I'm home!"

The kitchen door opened and his mother and father were standing there, waiting for him.

He stopped running, then, and looked at them, trying to

decide what to say, how to let them know how glad he was to be home.

"We ran logs over the Grand Falls, Pa, and Paddy McGarrity says logging men will be talking about us for years to come!" He laughed. "They'll be talking about us all, about the Main John and Paddy McGarrity and Shogomoc Sam Campeau."

Then he put his father's peavey where it belonged, beside the door, and went into the house where *he* belonged.

... Shogomoc's a-running wild,
Tobique's white with foam,
Once again the mighty drives
Are sluicing grandly home....

They sing songs about them and they tell stories about them and when the lone moose calls along the shores of the Squatook Lake and the logs are roaring down the river, they remember how it used to be ...

The Main John is a loggin' man and Shogomoc Sam is a loggin' man, too.

Oh, Shogomoc Sam isn't the giant the Main John was – there's only one giant and the Main John is that – but Shogomoc Sam is there, runnin' logs over the Grand Falls for the first time and marchin' into Maine, along the Allagash, and swingin' his pa's peavey hook as if it wasn't more than a bit of a pin.

And when loggin' men are tellin' stories about the Main John and how he used a tall pine for a toothpick and a towerin' maple for a pen holder, they talk about Shogomoc Sam, too, and how he set out to find his name and found out somethin' more instead.

"The Main John and Shogomoc Sam and the others – they're loggin' men, if ever there was one," they say in Fredericton and Saint John, and they sing songs and tell stories and remember how it used to be when loggin' men were kings.